Acknowledgment
The publishers would like to thank John Dillow
for the cover illustration.

Ladybird books are widely available, but in case of
difficulty may be ordered by post or telephone from:

Ladybird Books – Cash Sales Department
Littlegate Road Paignton Devon TQ3 3BE
Telephone 0803 554761

A catalogue record for this book is available
from the British Library

Published by Ladybird Books Ltd Loughborough Leicestershire UK
Ladybird Books Inc Auburn Maine 04210 USA

Printed in EC

About
building

by JACQUELINE HARDING
illustrated by STUART TROTTER

Ladybird

Two men came to measure the ground before the building began.

building

First a digger came
and scooped up
the earth.

digger

Everyone wore hard hats. Look out for that crane!

crane

Round and round went the cement mixer.

cement mixer

The bricklayers built the walls. What a lot of bricks!

bricks

The builders checked
the plans. The school
building was going well.

school

A bulldozer made the ground level.

bulldozer

A digger loaded
a tipper truck.

truck

Don't put glass
in the windows
yet!

windows

The roof was almost finished.

roof

The road roller made the playground smooth.

road roller

The painters painted inside and outside.

The school was ready for some children!